MONSTER ITCH

VAMPIRE TROUBLE

DON'T MISS ANY MONSTER ITCH BOOKS!

MONSTER ITCH

VAMPIRE TROUBLE

By David Lubar
Illustrated by Karl West

SCHOLASTIC INC.

Text copyright © 2017 by David Lubar
Illustrations copyright © 2017 Scholastic Inc.

ISBN 978-0-545-87349-9

10 9 8 7 6 5 4 3 2 1   17 18 19 20 21

Printed in the U.S.A. 40

First printing 2017

Book design by Mary Claire Cruz

For the staff and students of Spring Garden Elementary School in Bethlehem, PA, with special thanks to Dave Siegfried, Jane Cassidy, and Lauren Brennan for getting things started. Thank you for all the fun visits and great feedback over the years.

ONE

"Alex, stop looking out the window!" my teacher, Mrs. Fulmer, said.

"Sorry." I pulled my eyes from the window and tried to aim them toward the board, but they flickered past it to the clock above the door. I needed to see how close we were to recess.

"Alex!" she said. "Pay attention, or you'll get detention." She tried to frown at me to show she was serious but ended up fighting against a smile. I guess she'd realized she'd accidentally made a rhyme.

"Yes, Mrs. Fulmer." I forced myself to look straight ahead at the vocabulary words she'd written for the class. Detention would be just as bad as rain, since either one would keep me inside. And if I didn't get to go out, it would hurt my chance to do something amazing.

Luckily, my quick peek at the clock showed me we were only five minutes away from recess. And it didn't look like there'd be more rain, even though it rained last night and was still cloudy.

I glanced two rows over to my friend Stuart.

He held up five fingers with his right

hand and made a circle with his left thumb and forefinger. *Fifty.*

I flashed the signal back to him. *Fifty.*

The bell rang. I shot to my feet, along with everyone else.

"Wait," Mrs. Fulmer said.

We all froze and stared at her like dogs desperately eager to hear "Let's go for a walk."

"Dismissed," she said.

We rushed through the door and into the hallway, turning left for the exit that led to the playground.

"Fifty," Stuart said.

"For sure," I said. In all the years that kids had played kickball at Thomas Jefferson Elementary School, nobody had kicked fifty home runs in a single month. That's why I was watching the sky. If it rained, we'd have indoor recess. Then I wouldn't get to play kickball. I loved kickball. And I was good at it. I'd kicked forty-seven home runs this month. Forty-seven! I was within striking distance of setting a record. I wasn't the first to get close. In the past, five kids had reached forty-eight, and three had reached forty-nine. But fifty just didn't seem to happen. Maybe they'd all choked under the pressure of reaching such a perfectly round number. But I wouldn't.

I loved to compete at anything and everything. Sports, games, contests. And I loved to win. That kickball record was going to be mine. There were eight more school days left to the month. Nothing was going to stop me.

As I moved with the mob toward the door to the playground, I bumped into my cousin Sarah.

"You're always in such a rush," she said.

"I like recess," I said.

"We all do," Sarah said.

"But you've always had recess," I said. "It's still new for me."

We burst outside, and I inhaled a deep breath of the still-damp air. I loved the fact that damp air didn't make me cough. I really loved that my chest didn't hurt when I breathed. Until near the end of last year, I didn't get to go out for recess. I had really bad allergies. No matter what season, there was something that would make me cough, sneeze, itch, or wheeze. My mom— she's an allergy doctor—wrote me an excuse to get out of recess, even though I didn't want to be excused. I didn't get to go outside much after school, either. When I was stuck in my room, I used to put my pillow on the floor and kick it hard at a poster of a goalpost that I'd taped on the wall. I pretended I was scoring field goals. I guess all that kicking made a difference, since the first time I played kickball, I almost put one over the fence.

Happily, I was fine now. I no longer missed recess. I'd outgrown my allergies. Mom says that happens sometimes and that I was very fortunate.

As I stood there just beyond the door, thinking about how lucky I was, someone bumped into me from behind.

"Get out of my way, slowpoke," Herbert Clumpmeister said, running past me.

"He could catch you," Stuart said.

"No way." I tried to sound confident. But Herbert had scored forty-five home runs. If things went really badly for me, I could lose the record to him.

But that would never happen. I'd get to fifty before he did. That's what really mattered with records. It was *good* to reach fifty, but it was *great* to be the first one to do it.

"Have fun," Sarah said as she headed off toward the basketball courts.

"You too," I said. I cut over toward the ball field. There were puddles all over the place, including a huge one right near home plate, but the field was dry enough for us to play on.

"Hey, who's that?" Stuart asked as we lined up to reach into the bag that held the field positions. He pointed behind the backstop.

There was a young woman, or maybe she was an older girl, standing under the tree behind the backstop. I hadn't even noticed her. In her long black coat, floppy hat, and black pants, she sort of blended into the dark bark of the walnut tree. And it was hard to tell her age with her face hidden behind thick-framed sunglasses and droopy black hair. The little bit of her face that I could see was very pale, and she didn't look very happy.

"New monitor, I guess." Students from the local college earned extra money by helping keep an eye on things at the playground. Some retired people did that, too. They're all really nice, and they make sure nobody gets hurt.

I reached into the bag and plucked out one of the old tennis balls that was inside of it. THIRD BASE was written on it in permanent marker. That would be my starting position. We don't play two teams—we play a game where you rotate through all the field positions. Then you line up to wait for your turn to kick after you play right field. If the batter kicks a pop fly and someone catches it, they swap positions. And if the batter is out any other way—through a tag, a force, or being hit by the ball (everyone's favorite method)—he becomes the pitcher.

We took our positions. Herbert was up to bat first. He's pretty competitive, too. He pointed at me and said, "Watch out. I'm about to crush your chances for the record."

He didn't. Not this time.

As I moved through the outfield positions, from left to center to right, I watched

-9-

the new monitor. Most of the monitors get interested in the games, and even clap and cheer when someone makes a good play, or say comforting words when things go wrong, but Gloomy Girl just stood there, staring straight ahead as if we were no more interesting than stalks of corn or specks of dust.

Glancing over my shoulder, I saw a monitor by the basketball court clapping for Sarah as she sank a jump shot from beyond the foul line. Another monitor was helping swing a jump rope for three kids. But I turned my attention away from them as I heard the unmistakable sound of the ball getting a solid kick. It was a grounder to second and an easy out. Which meant I was back in the batting line. Soon after that I was up.

As I jogged to the plate, I flashed the *fifty* sign to Stuart, who was now at shortstop. He flashed it back. After I took my position in the batter's box, I looked at the new monitor. She still stared straight ahead, as if I didn't even exist. Well, she'd get more interested when I kicked the ball into orbit.

Lindsay Waller, who was pitching, rolled the ball toward the plate. I took a step back. And another step. And another. And—well, I took five steps back in all. That's my patented hyper-special foolproof kickball home run technique. Five steps back as the ball is rolling and then a dash forward to meet it perfectly at the plate with a super-duper kick.

As I took my fifth step, my nose started to itch. I couldn't worry about that. I had a ball to blast for a home run. It was a perfect pitch, traveling with just the right amount of speed for me to clobber it. That would put me at forty-eight!

I dashed forward. The itch filled my whole nose. *Ignore it*, I told myself. I reached the plate, planted my left foot firmly at the same time as I swung my right foot back. (I'm a lefty when I write or throw, but I kick righty.) The big secret to kickball is that you don't just kick with your foot, or even your leg. You kick with your whole body working together. I put my shoulder into it, and then my hip, followed by my knee. With the force of all my moving parts behind it, I unleashed a mighty kick. At the same instant, I sneezed so hard I thought my head would leave my neck.

When your head is sneezing and your foot is swinging, and the dirt around home

plate is just a little bit wet and slippery, things don't always go as planned. I missed the ball. I'd totally muffed the kick. Worse, I swung my leg so hard, I sent myself sailing through the air. And even worse than that, I was sailing right toward the huge mud puddle.

TWO

Splash! It was not a happy landing. I ended my fall poorly. And wetly.

Pretty much everyone on the field, and anyone off the field who saw my splash-down, was laughing.

"Strike one," Herbert said from his spot at second base.

"No fooling," I muttered as I pushed myself up from the muck. I could feel my face flushing. If it got any hotter, it would steam off the muddy water that was all over my neck and forehead. After I stepped back to the plate, I glanced at the monitor, just to prove to myself that I had to be wrong. Was she really totally uninterested in what had just happened? I'd done a face-first full-body plant in a mud puddle! I know a towel would be too much to ask, but a look of sympathy, or maybe an "Are you okay?" would have been nice.

But she didn't seem to react at all.

On the next pitch, as I backed up, I felt the itch again, on the third step. As I finished my five steps and started my dash, I felt another sneeze coming.

I gritted my teeth.

I'm not sneezing, I told myself.

I sneezed. This one was even harder. And, yeah, I went flying, again. And, naturally, I landed in the puddle, again. But I'd already soaked up most of the mud on my first fall, so this one didn't make things all that much worse.

Still, it seemed to draw even more laughter.

"Strike two," Herbert said.

I had no idea why I kept sneezing. But I realized that maybe this wasn't the time to try for a home run. I'd have plenty of chances to score the three homers I needed.

I sneezed on the fourth step as I backed up. And then I sneezed a second time as I moved forward. But I didn't try to nail the ball—I just sort of lashed my foot out at it and hoped to make contact. I actually made a solid hit. Unfortunately, it was also a weak one, popping up toward second base.

The ball dropped right into Herbert's hands. I could hear sighs of disappointment from all around the playground as I failed to land in the puddle again. Then I sighed because not only was I out, but thanks to catching my pop fly, Herbert was up. I was supposed to take his spot on the field, but I was just too muddy and discouraged to keep playing.

"Someone sub for mc," I said. I needed to wash off.

As I walked away, the ball smacked the back of my head with a loud *POING*!

I turned around and instantly spotted the ball's source. Herbert had kicked it right at me.

"Oops, sorry," he said, grinning. "Accident."

"Yeah, right." I didn't believe him. I watched the next pitch, so he wouldn't hit me again. Instead, he nailed the ball for a home run. Great. Really totally wonderful and great. I was a mud ball, and Herbert was within one home run of catching me.

I went inside to the art room and used the sink to clean up my face and arms. The art teacher, Mr. Pemberton, had a bunch of old shirts he kept on hand for kids to wear when they painted. He let me borrow one.

I had lunch right after recess.

"What happened to you?" Sarah asked when she saw me walking past the table where she sits with the other girls from the science club. Even with the clean shirt, I was pretty much a mess.

"I sneezed so hard, I flew into a mud puddle," I said.

Sarah laughed. "Wish I'd seen it. That must have been one monster of a sneeze."

As the words left her mouth, her eyes widened. She stared at me. I stared back at her. My eyes widened, too.

"No way," I said. Just the other week, after not having any allergies for a long time, I had gotten a very itchy rash as an allergic reaction to a ghost. But a sneeze wasn't a rash. And there was no ghost on the playground. At least, I was pretty sure

Gloomy Girl wasn't a ghost. She wasn't transparent.

But she sure was spooky.

"You're right," Sarah said. "One sneeze doesn't mean anything. Everyone sneezes."

I didn't tell her that it was more than one.

After school, when Sarah and I were heading out, I saw Gloomy Girl standing beneath a tree by the curb. The sky was still overcast, but the sun had peeked through a hole in the clouds.

I pointed to her and said to Sarah, "She was by the kickball field today. Maybe she's making me sneeze."

"That's silly," Sarah said. "Like I told you at lunch, one sneeze doesn't mean anything."

I confessed I'd sneezed three or four times.

"It could be her perfume or something," Sarah said. "Aunt Esther's perfume makes me sneeze."

I shuddered at the thought of that. "Aunt Esther's perfume kills insects and wilts flowers," I said. "I think she pours it on with a ladle. But, as terrible as it is, it has the same effect on everybody. I was the only one on the field who sneezed. And I only sneezed when I was near Gloomy Girl."

The hole in the clouds closed up, erasing the sunlight that painted the pavement. Gloomy Girl ran down the sidewalk, heading right toward us. I froze. As she got close, my nose itched and twitched. I turned toward Sarah to tell her what was happening. Just as Gloomy Girl sped past me, I sneezed, even harder than before. It happened so quickly, I didn't have time to turn away or cover my nose.

"Ew . . ." Sarah said as she reached toward her face. Little snot droplets glistened on her cheeks like flecks of quartz.

"Sorry," I said. "But see? She made me sneeze."

Sarah nodded. By the time she'd wiped her face and stopped saying "ew," Gloomy Girl was half a block away

Sarah and I looked at each other.

"Something weird is going on," I said. "How could I be allergic to a person?"

"Let's find out," Sarah said. She raced after Gloomy Girl.

"Actually, I'm not sure I want to know," I muttered, but I joined in the chase.

THREE

We closed the distance and got within about twenty feet of Gloomy Girl before she turned a corner. For a moment, we couldn't see her past the hedges that lined a front yard.

Then we sped around the corner . . . but Gloomy Girl wasn't there.

"Where'd she go?" I asked.

Something fluttered past us.

Sarah screamed.

I guess I did, too.

Something large and dark flitted right above our heads and then shot away, flying over the rooftops.

"A bat!" I said.

"In the daytime?" Sarah said. "No way. Bats are nocturnal. That was a bird."

Maybe she was right. Either way, I didn't feel like arguing. "Where'd Gloomy Girl go?" I stared down the street. There was no sign of her.

"Maybe she went into one of the houses," Sarah said.

"Maybe . . ." I didn't want to think that she'd vanished.

We headed toward home. Sarah lives just one block from me, which is convenient when I want to hang out with her and a nuisance when I don't.

"I hate the idea that my allergies are coming back," I said. I remembered all those days when I looked out the classroom window at everyone having fun at recess.

"That wouldn't be good," Sarah said. "Hey, I just thought of something . . ."

"What?" I asked.

"Maybe Gloomy Girl is a ghost!" Sarah said.

"I thought of that," I said. "I don't think she is—and this is sneezing, not a rash. I hope it doesn't get any worse, though, the way that the rash did." I definitely didn't want to sneeze any harder than I'd already sneezed.

"I don't blame you. But I guess we shouldn't jump to any conclusions," Sarah said. Then she laughed and added, "Or into more puddles."

"Very funny," I said.

Mom was in the living room reading one of her allergy-doctor magazines when I got home. Mom and Dad try to make sure one of them is there right after school every day. I don't know why. I can find the fridge without any help, and I understand the TV remote better than either of my parents.

"Alex!" Mom gasped. "You're covered in mud!"

"It's not that bad," I said. I'd actually pretty much forgotten about it. "And I wouldn't really call myself *covered*. A lot

of it flaked off already." I wrinkled my
forehead and watched a sprinkling of tiny
mud flakes flutter past my eyes. They were
kind of pretty, though not as glisteny as
snot droplets.

Mom knelt, lifted my eyelids with her
thumbs, and peered into my eyes. Then she
made me open my mouth and say *ahhhh*.
After that, she grabbed her stethoscope

and listened to my lungs. Once she was satisfied I wasn't in the middle of a severe allergy attack, she said, "Go clean up, immediately. Do you have any idea how many allergens and pathogens are in the soil?"

"Seven thousand six hundred ninety-four?" I guessed. I wasn't even sure what pathogens were.

"Don't be a wise guy," she said. "Just go get cleaned up."

She was waiting in the hall when I came out of the bathroom. "Here," she said, handing me a spirometer. That tests lung power. I took it, breathed into it, sent the little ball inside all the way to the top with a satisfying CLACK, then handed it back to her. "See? I'm fine," I said. "Really. I've got lungs like a lumberjack."

"We can't be too careful," she said. But she headed out for her office, after making me promise not to ever get muddy again.

That wasn't a problem the next day. The sun was shining hot and bright, and the puddles were gone from the playground. So was Gloomy Girl. But something else was there—a lingering memory of yesterday's disaster and a little bit of worry that history would repeat itself. That's not a good recipe for home runs. When I came up for my turn at the plate, I kept thinking about those sneezes. Every time I backed up my five steps, I waited for my nose to start itching.

My nose didn't itch. Not even once. I didn't sneeze. But all the worrying threw my timing off, and I didn't kick a home run, either.

Instead, someone else made a mighty kick. On his last turn, Herbert smacked a solid shot that arced high over the field toward the fence. Where I use skill and technique to strike the ball, Herbert is all about brute strength. He doesn't have much control (except when he's aiming at my head, I guess), and his kicks usually go all over the place. But when they go straight, they also go far.

"I got it!" Stuart shouted as the ball sailed above the infield. There was no way he'd get there in time. At least, that's what I thought as I watched the ball and Stuart move toward each other. But he put on a burst of speed, made a jaw-dropping leap, and snagged the ball with one hand right before it went over the fence.

"Thanks," I said as we headed in for lunch. "That was an amazing catch."

"I've got your back," he said.

"No sneezies?" Sarah asked when I walked past her table in the cafeteria.

"Achoo!" I said, aiming a fake sneeze at her.

"Very funny." She turned her attention to her food.

When we got back to class, I turned my attention to Mrs. Fulmer, because she had written something awesome on the board: FIELD DAY.

"I'll be passing out sign-up sheets," she told the class as soon as we took our seats. "Each of you has to pick three events."

I hadn't been allowed to compete in field day last year, because of all my allergies. That was rotten. But this year, I was allergy-free! I definitely wanted to be part of field day. It was where the whole school competed in all sorts of athletic events. You got points for how well you did in each of the ones you entered. The kids who got the most total points would get trophies. And trophies were awesome.

When I got my sheet, I looked at my choices. It was easy enough to pick three. I chose kickball, of course, where you could earn points for both kicking and fielding. I also chose the hundred-yard dash and the football distance throw. I was pretty fast at short distances. And, just like a good kick depends on using your body in a coordinated way, so does a good throw. I probably wouldn't throw the farthest, or run the fastest, but I figured the dash and the throw were my best chances to score a lot of points, to

add to the points I'd get in kickball. I could already
picture the trophy
I'd win on my
dresser at home.

"Ahem!"

I looked up.
Mrs. Fulmer was
standing there,
waiting for me to hand in my slip. I gave
it to her, then looked over at Stuart. I
kicked my foot, pumped my arms like
a runner, and then made a football-
throwing motion, letting him know my
choices.

Stuart kicked, shot a basket, and then
jerked his body sideways.

"So you're doing kickball, basketball,
and touching an electric eel?" I asked as

we headed out at the end of the day. I mimicked his jerky actions.

"High jump," he said. He made the motion again, and I realized it was his impression of someone sailing over the crossbar on his back, like they do in the Olympics.

"Are you signed up?" Sarah asked when I met her outside.

"Yup," I said. "Are you?"

"Foul shots, soccer dribbling—obstacle course, and hundred-yard dash," she said.

"I'm doing the dash, too," I said.

"You'll lose," she said.

"No I won't."

"I'm faster," she said.

"I'm more determined," I said.

"That has yet to be determined," she said. She grinned, to let me know she was sort of kidding about beating me. But she was right about being faster. Not that I'd admit it to her.

"Make way for speedy!" Herbert shouted as he raced past us down the walkway.

"I don't care who wins," I said, "as long as it's not him."

"Agreed," Sarah said.

We headed for our homes.

"I love this weather," Sarah said. "Too bad it won't last."

"How do you know?" I asked.

"I checked the forecast," Sarah said. "Tomorrow will be cloudy, again."

"Rain?" I asked.

"No, just clouds," Sarah said.

It turned out she was right. It was cloudy the next day when I woke up. I headed off for school, hoping that I'd be able to score at least one home run during recess. This was starting to remind me of when I had a whole week to write a paper, or a whole month to make a Halloween costume. And then, the next thing I knew, I had only a day left to do it and no idea where all the time went. I didn't want my chances to break the record to melt away like that.

At recess, I saw that Gloomy Girl was back beneath the tree behind the ball field. When I walked up to the plate, I gritted my teeth, clamping down as if I could cut off any sneezes that tried to escape from my lungs. On the first pitch, as soon as I backed up a step, my nose itched. By the second step, I sneezed, even though I tried my hardest not to. That was followed by two more quick sneezes. I tried to stop.

I tried to catch my breath. But I couldn't stop sneezing. With each sneeze, my lungs got emptier. I couldn't get any air back into them.

I felt like I was going to pass out.

FOUR

I staggered forward, still sneezing. When the ball reached me, I flailed my foot at it and made the weakest kick in the history of Thomas Jefferson Elementary School playground kickball. The ball dribbled down the first-base line, right into the hands of Jennie Oklum, who scooped it up and bounced it off my leg. I was out. I went to the pitcher's mound to take up my field position as the pitcher moved to first and Jennie moved to second. I'd stopped sneezing, but my nose and lungs felt like I'd inhaled a gallon of ocean water. Or maybe vinegar.

As other kickers came up to the plate and I made my way around the infield positions, I watched Gloomy Girl. She might as well have been a statue. Except for her hair moving slightly whenever the breeze picked up, she was totally still.

I was at third base when Stuart kicked a pop fly right in my direction. Instinct made me hold out my arms and back up so I'd be in the perfect spot to make the catch. Then I hesitated. If I caught the ball, I'd be up at the plate again. And if I was up, I'd start sneezing and make another terrible kick. Maybe I should let the ball bounce. I could still have time to field it and make the play at first. And I wouldn't have to go to the plate. I'd just move to the outfield.

No!

I hated the idea that I was even thinking about not playing my best. I turned my attention back to the game and caught the ball. "Sorry," I said to Stuart as I jogged past him to exchange positions.

"Don't be sorry. It was a good catch," he said.

"Thanks."

I walked up to the plate from in front. I knew I'd sneeze if I got closer to Gloomy Girl—I definitely seemed to be allergic to her. Even without backing up toward her, my nose itched a little. Just as I'd feared, I seemed to be getting more and more sensitive to her. I hoped that if I kept my distance, I could at least make a decent kick. I might even be able to score a home run, if I put all my strength into the effort.

The pitcher rolled the ball.

I stepped back.

Yeah. I know. I didn't want to step back. I told myself not to step back. I had a very good reason not to step back. It was a very bad idea to step back. Nobody in my position would ever dream of stepping back. I had to be a complete fool to step back. And yet, I stepped back. It was a habit—it was what I did every time. Including this time.

I sneezed. Kids around the field laughed. A couple of them stopped laughing long enough to mock me with fake sneezes. I rushed forward and kicked the ball. It went foul. So did my next kick. The third kick

didn't go foul—because I totally missed the ball. I struck out.

I.

Struck.

Out.

Of all the horrors I'd faced in my life, and all the horrors I might face down the road, nothing would ever come close to being as horrifying as this. Nobody ever strikes out in kickball. Nobody. It's a huge red ball. I could kick it with my eyes closed. At least, I could do that if I wasn't struggling to break the habit of stepping back at the same time I was fighting to keep from sneezing.

"Strikeout king!" Herbert shouted as I walked off the field. "Alex has the record for the most strikeouts ever!" He collapsed on the ground laughing.

I was supposed to go take up my position as pitcher, but I just said, "Substitute," and left the field. The dark clouds overhead were nowhere near as dark as the clouds that filled my mind and colored my mood.

I crossed the playground and went over to the basketball courts. Sarah was driving toward the basket. She fired a pass to one of her teammates, cut across the lane, got the ball back, and made a perfect lay-up.

I caught her eye. I guess she could tell I seriously needed her help, because she came right off the court. "What's wrong?"

"I don't know." I pointed at Gloomy Girl. "Just go take a look at her. I can't get close without having a sneezing fit. See if there's anything strange about her."

"Sure. I know all about *strange*. That's one of the benefits of being related to you." She trotted off toward the backstop. Sarah might kid me, and she might play the meanest possible jokes on me once in a while, but when it came to really important stuff, I could always count on her. And she could count on me.

I watched as she walked right up to Gloomy Girl and said something. Gloomy Girl didn't seem to notice her. Sarah spoke again. Gloomy Girl turned her head toward Sarah. I could tell she still hadn't said anything. A moment later, after what seemed like a very one-sided conversation, Sarah ran back toward me.

When she reached me, she was panting. But something else was going on. Sarah wasn't just winded. She was trembling. And her face was almost as pale as Gloomy Girl's.

"What's wrong?" I asked.

Sarah opened her mouth to speak, then closed it and shook her head, as if the words she wanted to tell me were too horrible to allow out of her throat.

"Take your time," I said.

Sarah nodded. I saw her body jerk, like someone had slapped her hard on the back. She shook her head again, as if trying to fling images free from her mind.

"I tried to talk to her," she said.

"I saw that," I said.

"She ignored me. I tried again. She looked at me and said, 'Go away.' There was something in her voice that made me shiver. I didn't even see her mouth move. It was like she sent the words right into my mind."

"That's creepy," I said.

"But that wasn't the worst part," Sarah said.

I looked across the playground. I couldn't see anything to explain why Sarah was so upset.

"Something rustled in the tall grass behind her," Sarah said.

"What?"

"Rats . . ." Sarah said.

"Rats?" I asked.

"A whole lot of them," Sarah said.

She paused again. I waited for the rest, even though I was pretty sure I didn't want to hear it.

FIVE

The silence grew. Sarah stared toward Gloomy Girl, then turned away.

"Rats?" I asked after the silence, and my curiosity became unbearable.

In answer, Sarah's body jerked again. She was still trembling, but not as much. "Dozens of them. In the grass. Lined up and looking at me like they were waiting for a command. I heard more words. *They will chase you off.* And then a picture burst into my mind. I could see the rats leaping toward me. They were—"

She stopped, again, gasping as if the words she was trying to say had actually choked her. I put a hand on her shoulder. "That's okay. You don't have to tell me any more. I've heard enough—she's not human."

"That's for sure," Sarah said. "What are you going to do?"

"I need to stay away from her," I said. "She can't be here forever. Monitors come and go all the time."

"Right. I hope she leaves really soon," Sarah said. She shuddered again.

"Are you going to be okay?" I asked. I felt terrible that I'd sent her over there.

Sarah nodded. Then, to my surprise, she allowed a thin smile to cross her lips. "Monitor monster," she said. "That would be sort of funny if it weren't so . . ."

"Real?" I asked.

"Real," she agreed.

I thought about the ghost, who would have haunted my grandparents' place forever if Sarah and I hadn't helped it find peace. "What if Gloomy Girl doesn't go away?" I asked.

"Then we'll have to make her go away," Sarah said. "So, first of all, we need to figure out what kind of monster she is. Then we'll have some idea what to do."

"I'm pretty sure she's not a ghost," I said.

"Yeah—ghosts can't talk," Sarah said. "And they sure can't summon up an army of rats."

Sarah and I were the only people who could see the ghost we'd encountered at our grandparents' place, and that was only after we'd gotten magical powder in our eyes. "Do we *know* other kids can see her?" I asked. I sort of remembered Stuart had mentioned her. Or maybe I'd mentioned her to him. I wasn't sure.

"That's easy enough to find out," Sarah said.

Just then the bell rang, so we headed in for lunch. After we got in line at the cafeteria, Sarah looked at Stuart and said, "That new monitor is creepy."

"What new monitor?" Stuart asked. "I didn't see any new ones."

Sarah and I stared at each other. Our mouths dropped open.

"You don't see her?" I asked. "By the tree behind the backstop."

"Oh, you mean the *playground* monitor," Stuart said. "I thought we'd gotten a new video monitor in the computer lab or something like that. So I was sort of confused trying to understand how that could be creepy. I mean, you could have a creepy image on a monitor, from a horror movie or a zombie survival game, but that wouldn't make the monitor itself creepy. But that new playground monitor—yeah, she is kind of creepy."

So Gloomy Girl wasn't a ghost that only Sarah and I could see. I was pretty sure she wasn't any other kind of ghost, either.

After school, Sarah said, "Grandpa sent me a book of monsters. Come over and we'll look through it."

I hesitated. I really didn't like scary movies or scary books.

"Relax," Sarah said. "It just has drawings. And they're sort of cartoony. No photos or realistic drawings."

"Okay. Let's do it."

We went to her house, where her Mom, who works at home as a researcher for a law firm, greeted us. We grabbed a snack and then started leafing through *The Big Book of Monsters*, which had the sort of drawings you see on cereal boxes.

"I had no idea there were so many types of monsters," I said. Between mythology, folklore, and literature, there was a dizzying assortment of creatures. I pointed to a page with a drawing of a person turning into a dog. "Shapeshifter? Could that be her?"

"Maybe," Sarah said. She flipped the page. We both shuddered at the next picture. "Definitely not a harpy."

We looked at pictures of werewolves, cyclops, mummies, wyverns, anthropophagi (I think I have a new favorite word), and mutant insects. Based on the descriptions written beneath the pictures, none of the monsters seemed like a close match to Gloomy Girl, though a lot of them were equally creepy.

"Imagine if you have a different allergy to each monster," Sarah said. "You could have werewolf wheezes and swamp-creature coughs. That would be awesome."

"You mean awful," I said.

"Maybe both," she said. She laughed and shouted, "Mummy mumps!"

"Mumps isn't an allergy," I said.

"It's still funny. Hey, zombie zits! Hydra hiccups! Boogieman burps!"

I waited while she spat out a dozen more monster maladies. "Finished yet?" I asked after her laughter had faded.

"Yeah."

I tapped the open page, which showed a basilisk. "Can we get back to work?"

"Sure," she said.

"Hey," I said, pointing to the next page. "Ghosts." We both read the description.

"Some of that isn't true," Sarah said.

"But a lot of it is," I said. The book said a ghost had to stay in an area connected with it, which was true, but it also said a ghost who haunted one building couldn't go to a different building. And I knew that was wrong. "This is going to make things harder."

"It might be a good idea to list what we know about Gloomy Girl so far," Sarah said. "We'll look for the closest match, first, and then worry about how much of the description in the book is true."

I mentioned everything that came to mind. "She can stay very still. She doesn't seem to care what we do. She likes shade."

"She disappeared when we were chasing her," Sarah said.

"Or maybe she just ran very fast," I said. "We can't assume anything, since we didn't see what she did."

"Good point," Sarah said, patting my arm. "You're starting to think like a scientist. What else do we know?"

"She can talk to your mind," I said. I hesitated. I knew Sarah wouldn't want to be reminded about what had happened, but I also figured it was important to include it. "And she can control rats."

I saw Sarah's jaw clench, but she seemed to be okay. She turned the page, and we found ourselves face-to-face with a man in a black cape. He had bloodred eyes and fangs. There was a coffin behind him. Bats flitted across the top of the page, and rats skittered across the bottom.

"Vampire . . ." we both whispered. We read

the description. Most of it seemed to fit Gloomy Girl.

"She turned into a bat!" I said, thinking about the time we'd chased Gloomy Girl.

"But vampires can't come out in the daytime," Sarah said. "Sunlight destroys them. Everybody knows that. It's in all the movies I've seen."

"That's what I've always heard, too." I pointed to the book. "And it says so right here."

Sarah pointed to the next line in the book. "At sunset, they creep out of the coffin." She made a creaking sound I didn't appreciate and looked around with her eyes wide open.

"But the book was wrong about some of the ghost stuff," I said. "What if it's wrong about this, too? Everything else fits. Maybe vampires just have to stay out of bright sunlight—and that would be why Gloomy Girl only comes to the playground when it's cloudy." I looked out the window at the overcast sky and found myself wishing I lived in a place where it was always sunny.

"That makes sense," Sarah said.

"So we can stop looking at monsters?" I asked. I reached out to close the book. Even though the drawing was cartoonish, I was tired of seeing the bloodred eyes and razor-sharp fangs. My mind kept putting Gloomy Girl's face into the picture.

Sarah grabbed my wrist to stop me, but didn't answer. I could tell by the way her body had tensed up that she'd been struck by a thought that scared her.

"What is it?" I asked.

"Let's assume she's a vampire," Sarah said. "Okay?"

"Okay. I think that's reasonable," I said.

"And some things we've heard about vampires are true, but other things aren't."

"Right. That's what we've found out."

"So, there's the one big thing about them that everybody knows," Sarah said. "And I really hope it isn't true, even though it's in the book."

As she spoke, I realized what she'd been thinking about. As all of this sank in, the room suddenly felt ten degrees colder. "If it's true," I said, "she's there at the playground because she's waiting for a chance to drink our blood."

SIX

"That's horrible." Sarah shuddered and clutched her throat, as if she were already imagining Gloomy Girl feasting on her blood.

"But we don't know if it's true," I said. "There has to be another way to verify it." I walked over to her computer and typed *vampires* into the search window.

"Ninety million results," Sarah said, reading over my shoulder. "You might want to call your folks and let them know you'll be busy for the next sixty-five thousand days."

I stared at her, wondering where that number came from.

"That's if we look at one site a minute," she said.

"It's impossible. There's no way we can sift through all the information," I said. "And misinformation," I added, remembering last month when Mr. Donlevy, our school librarian, had given us a lesson where he showed how much of the information on the Internet was incorrect or unreliable. It was scary how easy it was for people to post anything they wanted.

"Wait!" Sarah grabbed my shoulders. She does that when she gets excited about an idea. The bigger the idea, the sorer my shoulders will be for the next day or two. Based on the pain, this was a huge idea.

"Let's search for what we already know is true," she said.

"Huh?" I didn't follow that. "Why do we need to find what we already know?" I asked.

"Because, if an article has all the stuff we know is true and nothing that we know for sure is false, it's more likely that the rest of the stuff in it is also true. Get it?"

It took me a moment, but then I saw what she meant. "That's pretty smart," I said. "It's like if someone has never lied to you, that makes it easier to believe them the next time they tell you something."

"Exactly!" Sarah said.

Next to where I'd already typed *vampire*, I added all the things we'd seen or suspected. *Turns into a bat. Summons rats. Needs shade. Can go outside in the daytime.* We still got a lot of hits, so I narrowed it down even more as Sarah offered suggestions like *emotionless*. She really knew how to do research.

Eventually, we found ourselves with just a handful of websites in the results list. I copied everything that all the sites agreed on. I was happy to learn that even though vampires could drink blood, they didn't need it to survive. And I found an explanation for how Gloomy Girl could be at the playground during recess. It turned out vampires used to be able to come out only at night. But over the centuries, they'd found ways to survive outside on cloudy days. They still had to avoid direct sunlight. When the sun was out, they couldn't just stay indoors. They had to seek shelter in a coffin filled with their native soil. That was a little creepy, but the scariest part was another sentence: *They have almost no human emotions but can be driven to rage.* I decided not to think about that part right now.

"They hate the smell of garlic," Sarah said as we studied the list. "Maybe you can drive her off."

"It's worth a try," I said.

"Of course, if she can stand your regular breath, I'm not sure garlic would make all that much of a difference." Sarah laughed at her own joke.

"Very funny," I said.

"I thought so," Sarah said. She pointed at our list. "At least we know what we're dealing with. That's a good thing."

"Thanks for helping," I said as I headed out.

Right before dinner, Mom dumped my backpack on the living room floor. She does that once a week, to see what papers I brought home. I sort of forget to give them to her sometimes.

"Field day," she said to Dad as she held up the flyer. "This is wonderful. We have to go."

"Absolutely," Dad said. "It will be fun watching Alex compete."

An image sprang to mind of Mom and Dad clapping and cheering as I kicked home runs. But a shadow fell across that image as clouds filled the sky and Gloomy Girl joined the other playground monitors. I pictured Mom and Dad watching me walk up to the plate. I saw myself sneezing uncontrollably. I imagined Mom snatching me up and dragging me off to her office, where I would be dosed with all sorts of medicines and forbidden to participate in any more sports. She might even ban me from going outside.

"It's not a big deal. I don't think many parents are coming," I said.

"Well, we'll certainly be there," Mom said. "Don't you worry about that."

I added that to my list of worries. But that night, as I was going to sleep, I got an idea. I still had all sorts of allergy medicines. Was there one that would keep me from sneezing?

I knew I wasn't supposed to take medi-cine without telling Mom, or some other adult, though. That was a pretty big rule, and it was definitely a rule I wasn't going to break. But it was overcast again the next day, which meant I had to take a risk of a different kind. A huge risk.

In the morning, while we were sitting at breakfast, I sneezed. It was a very small sneeze. It was also a very fake sneeze, but it got Mom's attention.

"Are you all right?" she asked.

I sniffed once, frowned, then said, "I think so." A minute later, I faked another sneeze.

"It could be a delayed reaction to that mud. Let's not take any chances," Mom said. She opened the cabinet above the kitchen sink where she kept some of the medicine. "Here. Just in case. This should stop you from sneezing, but it won't make you sleepy."

I took the pill she handed me and swallowed it with a gulp of my grape juice. "Thanks. I'm sure this will take care of things," I said after Mom had checked my eyes, ears, and lungs.

"We'll keep a close eye on you," she said.

"Great."

Before I headed off to school, I grabbed a clove of garlic from the basket on the kitchen counter. Between the medicine that I hoped would keep me from sneezing and the garlic, which I hoped would help drive off the vampire, I figured my problems were solved.

For the first time since Gloomy Girl appeared, I was excited for recess. Right before my turn at the plate, I pulled the garlic out of my pocket. When I reached the plate, I held it up. Gloomy Girl didn't even blink. Maybe I was too far away. I remembered what Sarah had said.

Of course, if she can stand your regular breath, I'm not sure garlic would make all that much of a difference.

Maybe I could hit her with a blast of garlic breath. It was worth a try. I popped the garlic in my mouth and started chewing.

Oh, good golly . . .

I liked garlic when it was cooked into spaghetti sauce or chopped and baked on garlic bread. But a hunk of raw garlic is a dreadful thing to chew on. No wonder vampires hate it.

Fighting the urge to gag, I turned toward Gloomy Girl and exhaled in her direction like I was blowing out the world's largest birthday candle.

She actually blinked. And she took a half step back. That was good. But I realized my nose still itched. The medicine Mom gave me had no effect on my monster allergy. That was bad. Even worse, the garlic didn't drive Gloomy Girl far enough from me to keep me from sneezing. Her allergy effect had a larger range than my garlic blast. I could tell that if I stayed where I was, I'd be sneezing very soon.

Too late, I realized I should have just tossed the garlic toward her. There was nothing I could do about that now. I walked off the field. It was bad enough I'd never get my chance to score those last three home runs. Even worse, I knew field day would be a disaster for me if I tried to play kickball and had a sneezing fit while my parents were around. I had to change my sign-up sheet. There was only one way to do that. I didn't like the idea, and it scared me almost as much as facing a monster, but I had no choice.

SEVEN

I headed for the cave where the troll lived. Okay, it wasn't a cave. It was the basement of the school. And he wasn't a troll. He was my gym teacher. But he was big and loud and just a little bit scary. Maybe that's why they put his office underground.

The door was open. He was sitting there at his desk, dressed in blue sweatpants and a gray sweatshirt that was stretched tight against his huge muscles.

"Excuse me, Mr. Stompbruiser. Can I ask you something?"

He looked up from a chart that covered half his desk. There were pens and pencils scattered all around him. "What?" he growled.

I took a step back. "I'd like to switch from kickball to . . ."

I realized I hadn't picked the event I wanted to switch to.

"Spit it out!" he said.

"Um . . ."

"Be decisive! He who hesitates is lost." He smacked his desk with his fist. "Get to the point."

"The long jump," I shouted. That was the first thing that came to mind. I wasn't all that good at jumping high, long, or any other direction, but by now I didn't care. I just needed to get out of kickball so my Mom wouldn't see me having a sneezing fit.

"You want to switch from kickball to the long jump on field day?" he asked.

"Yeah. Please." I was glad he understood what I wanted.

"Absolutely not!" he shouted. "I've spent hours scheduling everything and everyone. There is no way I'm making any changes at this point."

"What if I found someone who would swap with me?" I asked. "Then, you'd just have to switch two names."

His glare was all the answer I needed. He turned away from me and went back to the chart. I was about to leave when I spotted another sheet of paper on a clipboard on his desk. This was regular size, with a line printed at the top in big letters: PLAYGROUND MONITOR SIGN-UP SHEET. Beneath that, there were names and assignments for today. I saw Mr. Halpern, the retired guy, was listed, as always, for jump rope. I scanned the rest of the list and noticed something about Gloomy Girl that, despite the mess I was in, made me laugh.

"What's so funny?" Mr. Stompbruiser asked.

"Nothing." I turned toward the door. There was no way I could explain it to him. My laugh got louder as I walked down the hall, until it was as out of control as my sneezes. I couldn't remember the last time I'd laughed like this. It felt good. I guess my brain—and my body—needed some relief.

Gasping for breath, I headed to the library. When I got online, I used what I'd just learned to search for information about Gloomy Girl. I also checked the news in town for events that might be connected with a vampire. I didn't find anything. But one article caught my eye. The headline read: *Local Shipping Company Offers Bicycle as Prize for Slogan Contest.*

According to the article, the company, which used to just handle local deliveries with bicycle messengers, was expanding into a worldwide delivery service. They needed a new slogan, since their old one, *We Pedal Your Packages Perfectly*, no longer fit.

I can do better than that, I thought as I clicked the link to the contest page.

I love contests, and I love bicycles. My bike is in pretty bad shape. It would be awesome to win a new bike. I thought about shipping. A slogan hit me. I typed it in: *When it comes to shipping, we deliver!* Not bad. I filled out the entry form and clicked SUBMIT.

The bell rang. I headed for the cafeteria. I couldn't wait to tell Sarah what I'd discovered. When I reached her I said,

"I saw the daily playground monitor sign-up sheet. You'll never guess what Gloomy Girl's first name is."

"Draculina?" Sarah guessed.

"Not even close. Want to guess again?" I asked.

"No. Just tell me."

"It's Pepper," I said.

Sarah smiled. "You're kidding."

"Nope. I just saw it. Pepper Moroaica. She probably made it up. When I tried to look up that name, I found out that *Moroaica* is a Romanian word for a female vampire." I shook my head. "I couldn't help laughing at her first name."

Sarah laughed, too. "It is kind of hilarious. Pepper makes you sneeze!"

I told her I'd tried and failed to get out of kickball. "Any ideas?" I asked. "You know what will happen when my mom sees me sneezing."

"We'll think of something," Sarah said.

I hoped so.

When I got home from school, Mom was waiting for me. As soon as I stepped inside, she asked, "How is your sneezing?"

Sneezing?

I felt like my brain had been kicked in the gut. I know that makes no sense, but that's the best I can do.

How did she know about my vampire allergy?

My mind raced in a desperate search to find something to say. As I smacked into blank walls in panic, some tiny calm part of my brain whispered, *You pretended to sneeze this morning. Remember?* Oh, yeah. Right. That's why she was asking about my sneezing.

"I'm fine," I said. That was true. I hadn't sneezed at school because I hadn't gotten close enough to Gloomy Girl, who I really didn't want to start thinking of as Pepper.

"Well, we'll just keep a careful eye on you," Mom said. "Especially when you're outdoors."

This was just getting better and better. I'd probably end up spending the rest of my school years in my bedroom, staring out the window at bright sunny skies. Because I knew that the moment I was yanked out of recess, there would never again be even one cloudy day.

That night, at dinner, I took another shot at convincing my parents they didn't want to go to field day. I failed.

After dinner, as it was getting dark, Mom said, "I need to drop off my books at the library. Want to come for a ride?"

"Sure!" I loved our town library. And there was an ice cream shop right next to it. I knew I had a pretty good chance of convincing Mom to stop there on the way home.

We got in the car and headed across town.

"I should have taken the highway," Mom said right after we turned onto Lake Street.

I looked out the window. Traffic was backed up ahead of us. We crawled. I didn't mind. We'd still get to the library way before they closed.

Then my nose started to itch.

Oh, no. If I sneezed again, after sneezing twice this morning, Mom would be totally convinced my allergies were coming back, and then she'd definitely go into doctor mode when I sneezed a ton of monster sneezes at field day, if she even let me participate at all.

I looked around and had to bite back a gasp. It was *her*. Gloomy Girl was walking toward us from behind, moving slowly along the sidewalk. She was far enough away so the itch was still just a little tickle. But I knew if it grew any stronger, there was no way I could hold back a sneeze.

The car moved. My nose felt better.

"Sit straight, Alex," Mom said. "You'll wreck your posture if you keep twisting around like that."

I sat straight. The car stopped again. I looked in the side-view mirror. Gloomy Girl was getting closer. The itch came back.

I reached out and turned the radio on, cranking the volume so Mom wouldn't hear my sneeze.

"Alex! Do you want to lose your hearing?" she said. She turned the radio off.

The itch got worse. Gloomy Girl got closer. Finally, the traffic moved and we drove down the street fast enough to get way ahead of her. When we turned onto Park Street, with no traffic in sight, I let out a sigh of relief.

And I sneezed.

I guess all the exposure I'd just had to the vampire added up. And I'd let my guard down when I'd sighed.

"Alex!" Mom said. "Maybe I should take you back home."

"It's nothing," I said. "I think there's some dust in the car."

"Nonsense," Mom said. "There is no dust in anything we own."

She was right about that. But at least I knew that there wouldn't be another sneeze. Not today. But today wouldn't last forever. Field day was coming. Everything seemed hopeless.

When we got home, I grabbed another clove of garlic. Maybe it wasn't too late to toss a piece by the vampire's tree. "Okay if I go see Sarah?" I asked.

"Sure," Dad said. "Just be home before bedtime."

I headed out to her place. "I want to put this garlic where Gloomy Girl stands," I said when she answered the door.

"That could work," she said. "Let's try it."

As we crossed the playground, Sarah asked, "What if she's around?"

"There's no reason for her to be here," I said. "She's only around during recess."

"I wonder why she ever became a playground monitor?" Sarah said.

"Me too." I hadn't figured that part out.

I walked around the backstop and approached the tree.

Something rustled in the grass.

I knew what it was before I saw any of them.

Rats.

They reared up and stared at us. They were big. Some were almost the size of cats. They

dropped back on all fours and started to walk toward us. I guess Gloomy Girl had ordered them to guard her spot. It worried me that she seemed to have anticipated my move. She wasn't just a bloodsucking monster—she was a *smart* bloodsucking monster.

"Let's get out of here," Sarah whispered.

"Good idea." I backed away. The rats, much to my relief, remained where they were. I was pretty sure we could have outrun them if they'd charged at us, but I was happy not to find out for sure or add another nightmare experience to my collection.

When I was far enough from the tree that I felt safe, I threw the garlic at it. Maybe that would do the trick. But as soon as it landed, I saw a flurry of activity as the rats leaped onto it.

"I think they ate it," Sarah said.

"Better it than us," I said.

We walked back toward our homes. I realized there was only one more thing I could try. And it scared me even worse than talking to my gym teacher or facing a horde of rats.

EIGHT

At recess the next day, I walked over to a bench that was near the ball field but far enough from the tree that I wasn't in danger of sneezing. It was cloudy again, of course, and Gloomy Girl was in her usual place.

"Pepper?" I whispered.

I waited, wondering whether it would work. Vampires were supposed to have extraordinary hearing.

What?

The word drifted into my mind, echoing like it had been spoken in an empty tomb. I wasn't sure whether I was glad or unhappy that she'd heard me. Either way, I went on with my plan.

"You make me sneeze," I said.

So? If words had temperatures, that one was below freezing.

"My parents are coming for field day. They'll think I'm sick and keep me from going out for recess after that. And I can't play if you're standing there. I'm close to fifty home runs. I can't let Herbert beat me to the record. He's really annoying. If he beats me, he'll never shut up about it. It's the best record ever. I really need to get it. I've worked really hard. I'm so close."

You talk too much.

"Sorry." I realized I'd sort of been babbling.

I don't care about these mortal concerns.

"Can't you go somewhere else?"

No. This job suits me.

"But why do you need a job?" I asked.

I left my homeland. I thought I'd like it here. I don't. I need to earn money to go back to Transylvania. I miss Vistrincz, my village, and the safety of living with my fellow vampires at the Coffinmaker's Guild Hall there.

I remembered Mr. Halpern joking about how little he earned. "But they don't pay monitors a lot. It will take you forever to earn enough money to go home," I said.

I am patient. Forever *means nothing to me. Neither do you. Stop cluttering my ears with your pathetic words.*

"But it would just be for one day," I said.

Enough! Anger makes me thirsty. You've been warned.

It looked like there was no way she'd give me any sympathy. I guess because she had no sympathy to give. But I did have one last thing to ask. "Why did you pick the name Pepper?"

Because it's pretty.

That surprised me. Maybe she wasn't totally heartless. But she was close enough to emotionless that I knew I could never get her to do anything for me. I headed for the library.

I went to the library during recess again on Friday because the sun had totally abandoned me. There was no point in going to the field. I guess I could have played something else, but it made me sad to see everyone playing kickball without me. It would also have made me sad to see Herbert kick more home runs. It was bad enough hearing that he was now at

forty-nine. It would have been terrible to see him actually make those kicks. And it was going to be really terrible if he kicked number fifty during field day, and I had to watch it.

Saturday afternoon, I was sitting on my front porch when a guy came up the street on a bicycle. He had a messenger bag slung over his shoulder and was wearing a shirt from Speedy Fast Shipping Service. That sounded familiar. There was a car following him.

He coasted up the walkway. Then he hopped off the bike and pointed at me. "Are you Alex?" he asked.

"Yeah." I couldn't take my eyes off the bike. It was really nice.

"Congratulations," he said. "You're a winner."

"I am?!" I'd forgotten about the contest. "That's an awesome bike."

"It sure is," he said. "And I can't wait to deliver it to the first-prize winner."

As those words sank in, I watched him reach into a pouch and pull out an envelope. "Here's your prize. Congratulations on winning third place."

I took the envelope from him, then watched as he pedaled off on what was apparently not my bike. The car drove off, too. I guess that was how the guy would get back to work after he delivered the bicycle. I opened the envelope and pulled out the contents.

"Yippee," I muttered sarcastically as I read the certificate. I'd won one free delivery of a package up to ten pounds, anywhere in the country, every week for a year. I shoved the certificate back in the envelope, went upstairs, and put it on my desk in my room. This was useless. I was a kid. Kids don't send packages.

Kids get packages. That's how the world works.

As I was leaving my room, the phone rang. It was Sarah.

"I have an idea," she said.

"What?" I asked.

"I think we can find where the vampire lives," she said.

"How?" I asked.

"Come on over and I'll show you," she said.

I headed for Sarah's house. When I got there, I found her on the computer, studying a map. "Here's where we saw her when she was walking away from the school," Sarah said, drawing a line in the direction Gloomy Girl had gone. "And this is where you said you saw her walking along the sidewalk on your way to the library." Sarah drew a second line. Then she circled the spot where the lines crossed. "She probably lives in this area."

"Okay. So what if we find where she lives?" I said. "How does that help us?"

Sarah opened her mouth and then shut it. After a long silence, she said, "I hadn't thought it all the way through. I was just excited that I figured out how to find her. If we had a third sighting, we could even triangulate for greater accuracy. But I guess you're right. I didn't think things through far enough. I'm sorry I wasted your time." Her head drooped.

"Well, the part you did think of is very cool," I said. "You could definitely be a detective. Or a scientist."

She lifted her head a bit.

"I would never have figured out anything like that," I told her.

"Thanks. Hey, look on the bright side. Maybe it will be sunny on Monday," Sarah said.

"That would be a bright side," I said. "Do you think it might be?"

She pulled up a weather site on her computer, then pointed at the forecast on the screen. "Not a chance. It's going to be mostly cloudy."

"Mostly," I said. That word gave me the tiniest bit of hope. But as I left Sarah's house and looked up at the cloudy sky, all I could see was gloom.

She called me again Sunday evening. "Maybe there is a bright spot," she said. "I'm coming over."

When she came in, she held up her phone and said, "According to the forecast, the clouds might break for a little while, right around sunrise."

"So?" I asked.

"So she'll be in her coffin for sure. That's when it will be safe to try to keep her from leaving it."

"How?" I asked.

"I don't know. I figured we could brainstorm about it. Maybe we can find an answer if we think hard enough. You can't just give up!"

"I can't?" I shouted. "The whole universe has been telling me to give up. I'm allergic to a vampire who doesn't care if I sneeze. I'm losing the record to Herbert, who is one home run away from gloating at me for the rest of my life. My mom is about to lock me in the house forever. And just when I thought I'd won a really nice bicycle, I get the worst prize ever!"

I picked up the envelope and threw it at Sarah. "So, yeah, I give up."

Instead of saying anything, Sarah took the certificate out of the envelope. She frowned slightly as she read it. I guess she was learning just how useless my prize was. I was pretty sure she didn't have any packages to send. But then she smiled. "You didn't read the whole thing, did you?"

I shrugged. I was finished talking.

Sarah shoved the certificate in front of my face. I pushed her hand away.

"Alex," she said. "Stop acting like a spoiled brat. Read the whole thing."

I read it. And then I read it again, more carefully. And then it finally hit me. And then I smiled. "I'm so glad you noticed that. This just might work," I said.

"It might. But we're going to have to get really lucky," Sarah said.

"I'm about due for some luck," I said. "Especially when it comes to clouds. We better make plans."

"Absolutely," Sarah said. "Planning is the best way to get luck to show up."

We talked things over and figured out a good strategy. "Thanks," I said as she was leaving.

"Don't thank me until it works," she said.

"I might not be able to thank you if it doesn't," I said. I remembered Gloomy Girl's warning: *Anger makes me thirsty.* Tomorrow, I would be meddling with her life, which might end up making her angry.

NINE

A boom woke me. It was dark. I was confused for a moment. I checked my clock—sunrise was an hour away. And the boom was thunder. I heard rain hitting the roof and saw a series of lightning strikes hit not far off.

But the rain stopped about a half hour after that. I watched the sky and smiled when I saw a faint glow. The clouds had lifted.

"Ready?" I asked Sarah when I met her in front of her house. I'd left a note for my parents telling them I'd gone to school early to practice for field day.

"Ready," Sarah said. She headed down the street. I followed her. We walked toward the area where Gloomy Girl probably lived.

"You just have to pay real close attention to your nose," Sarah said.

"Right. I remember what we did last time," I said. We'd tracked the ghost a similar way.

And it worked again. By being aware of the tiniest possible tickles in my nose, I was able to narrow down the neighborhood and then the street. Finally, we found a house that had to be the right one. When I tried to get close, I started to sneeze.

"I can't go in," I said as I backed away. "You'll have to do it."

"I know," Sarah said. She took the certificate from me. But she didn't go toward the house.

"What's wrong?" I asked.

"I'm not sure it's right. I mean, I'd be breaking into a house."

"But not a person's house," I said.

"She's still a person," Sarah said. "Just a different kind."

"I guess you're right." I looked at the house. There was a garage next to it. The door was open. Maybe the lightning had triggered the opener. I looked up and down the street. A lot of garage doors were open. Then I returned my attention to the space in front of me. "Is that what I think it is?" I asked. I pointed inside, to something that looked very much like a coffin propped up on two sawhorses.

"Yeah," Sarah said. "It sure is."

"So a bit of luck finally did show up for me," I said. "I hope it brought some friends."

"Me too," Sarah said.

"What if she's not in there?" I asked.

"She has to be," Sarah said. She pointed at the sun. "She can't come out if it isn't cloudy." Sarah headed inside the garage and walked up to the coffin. She put her hand on it and gave it a push, then turned toward me and nodded. I guess it felt heavy enough that she knew Gloomy Girl was inside.

I checked the sky, hoping the sun didn't go away. I really didn't want Gloomy Girl to pop out of her coffin, see us, and get angry enough to drink my blood. Or Sarah's. My nose was still itching, so I moved even farther away.

Sarah taped the certificate on the coffin, along with a label addressed to the Coffinmaker's Guild Hall in Vistrincz. Then she called the shipping company and told them where to go to pick up the package. I was so glad she'd read the whole certificate. As I'd mentioned, it was for mailing a ten-pound package once a week for a year. But what I didn't see, because I'd stopped reading, was that it could also be used just once—to ship a package of up to 520 pounds anywhere in the world.

And that's what we were doing. Assuming the shipping company got there before the clouds returned and Gloomy Girl came out.

"Have a safe trip," Sarah said.

"I hope you like it when you get back home, Pepper," I said over my shoulder as Sarah and I walked away.

We got to school just in time. After Mrs. Fulmer took attendance, we all went outside for field day.

The sun was halfway hidden under the clouds by then. I saw Mom and Dad in the bleachers. They waved and cheered.

Herbert was wearing a sweatshirt with 50! written on it in black marker.

As I was moving toward the kickball field, I saw a Speedy Fast Shipping Company van go past, heading in the direction of Gloomy Girl's house.

After all the sneezes, gloom, mud, and rats, it was nice to finally feel that things might work out. I guess good thoughts are a good thing to have, because I snagged Herbert's first kick right before it could go over the fence. That stopped him from getting the record, earned me a place at the plate, and sent him to my spot in left field.

The good feelings continued as I kicked a home run. After rounding the bases, I took up my spot as pitcher. Herbert moved to center field.

Thanks to a pop-up when I was pitching, I got my second chance at the plate. And my second home run. I felt my whole body vibrate with the thrill of getting so close to my dream. I was tied with Herbert at forty-nine!

I saw my parents clapping as I moved back to the mound. On the field, Stuart was flashing the *fifty* sign. Kids all around the playground were paying attention to the game.

Just one more, I thought. I knew I could do that on my next turn at the plate.

But one thing still stood between me and the record. After the next batter grounded out, Herbert was on deck. Or maybe two things stood in my way. It had become totally cloudy. The sky was so dark now that I knew the sun wouldn't be coming out for a long time. I checked all around, afraid I'd spot Gloomy Girl heading toward me.

Stuart, who was up, kicked a home run. I was happy for him. But I hoped he hadn't started a trend, because it was now Herbert's turn. He walked up to the plate, pointed at me where I stood at second base, and shouted, "Say bye-bye to the record!"

The pitcher rolled the ball. Herbert grunted as he unleashed a brutal kick. The ball sailed along the third-base line. But it had a lot of spin, and it curved sharply. I smirked as I watched it sail into foul territory before going over the fence. But that was only strike one. Herbert would have at least two more chances, and even more if he kept kicking foul balls. I looked back at the plate and saw people rushing over to it.

Herbert was on the ground, clutching his leg. He'd pulled a muscle. He hobbled back to his feet and tried again. But he grounded out.

Herbert wasn't going to beat me to the record. All I had to do now was kick one more home run.

That's when my nose started to itch.

"Oh, no!" I said.

I looked around, knowing I'd see Gloomy Girl walking toward the tree. Or maybe walking toward me to unleash her anger.

x

But I didn't see her. Instead, I saw the Speedy Fast Shipping Company van heading the other way, toward the airport. That's why my nose itched. With luck, the coffin was headed back to Transylvania. Unless Pepper was angry enough about my meddling to burst free and show me what vampire rage was like.

On my next turn, I pushed all my fears and worries away . . . and kicked the hardest, farthest, most awesome scorcher ever, scoring both my fiftieth home run,

and the record for longest kick in the history of Thomas Jefferson Elementary. It felt amazing.

Kids all around the playground cheered. So did all the parents in the bleachers. Sarah, who was way over on the basketball court, yelled so loud I could hear her. After I rounded the bases, I walked behind the backstop and approached the tall grass. There was no sign of rats.

When kickball ended, I was so pumped up with excitement, I threw my best throw ever at the football competition and came in second. That made me feel even more amazing.

On my way to the track for the hundred-yard dash, I looked at the bench, where Herbert sat, rubbing his leg. I walked over, trying to think of something nice to say to him to make him feel better.

"Hey, congratulations," he said. He pulled off his sweatshirt and handed it to me. "I guess this is yours, now."

"Thanks." I took the shirt from him and put it on.

"Give me a hand," he said. "We have a race to run."

I helped him limp over to the track.

As we lined up, I looked over at Sarah, who had won the foul shooting and scored well at soccer. She looked back at me. "Herbert's having an awful day," I said.

"I know," she said.

"On your marks!" Mr. Stompbruiser called.

We got ready.

"Maybe we should . . ." I said.

"Definitely," Sarah said.

"Get set!"

We crouched.

"You sure?" I asked.

"I'm sure," she said.

"Go!"

Sarah and I dashed for the finish line. But we didn't run as fast as usual. We stayed behind Herbert. Everyone else blasted past him. When he crossed the finish line, his whole body slumped like he was being crushed by sadness. He must have figured he'd come in last. Knowing Herbert, he hated being last even more than he hated not being first. I guess I know that because I sort of feel the same way. At least, most of the time. But not now.

Herbert looked back just as Sarah and I crossed the finish line together, side by side in last place.

"What a pair of—" he said. I saw his lips start to form the word *losers*. But then he sort of jolted, like his conscience had poked his brain in the eye. And, yeah, I know that doesn't make much sense, either, but that's what it looked like. Instead of *losers*, he ended his sentence with, "awesome athletes and good sports."

When I saw the look of gratitude on his face, I felt great about holding back. I had my record. And, with no sign of Gloomy Girl beneath the tree, I had lots more kickball—sneeze-free kickball!—in my future. Who knew? Maybe I could kick sixty home runs next month.

"We did it," I said to Sarah.

She grinned. "We sure did."

Even with a last-place finish in the dash, I ended up with enough points for a trophy. Sarah got one, too. Mom and Dad took us out for ice cream after school.

"Well, that was certainly exciting," Dad said.

"And you didn't seem to have any trouble with your allergies," Mom said.

"Nope. No trouble at all," I said.

My sneezes were gone. At least, they were until two weeks later, when I went out to get the mail on a Saturday morning. As I pulled the envelopes and catalogs out of the box, my nose itched.

There was a black envelope on top of the stack, with my name and address written on it in red marker, and a familiar return address that I knew was for a guild hall in Transylvania.

I opened the envelope and sneezed. There was a card inside from Gloomy Girl. She wrote, "Thank you. Tell your friend I had safe travels." I guess she'd heard us in the garage and was glad we'd helped her get home. I told myself if I ever wrote a book about vampires, I'd be sure to say that they aren't totally heartless.

"You're welcome," I said as I put the card back in the envelope. It might make my nose itch, but I figured it was all right for me to keep it, as long as I didn't look at it while Mom was around. And it would be a good way to remember one amazing day when I'd helped a vampire, set a record, and did something nice for a person I didn't like. Or used to not like. Herbert's actually sort of okay, once you get to know him.

I jogged over to Sarah's house. When I got there, I showed her the card.

"Nice," she said.

"Yeah."

"I wonder what monster will be next— and what allergic reaction you'll have to it!" Sarah said with a grin.

"There won't be any more monsters," I told her. Though I sort of hoped I was wrong.

Don't miss Alex's first

MONSTER ITCH

When Alex and his cousin Sarah are visiting their grandparents, Alex gets a terrible red, itchy rash. Yikes! He's allergic to a ghost! Even worse, the ghost won't leave him alone—he wants Alex and Sarah's help. Can they solve the ghost's mystery and get rid of Alex's awful rash before it ruins everything?

NEVER LEAVE A BUG BEHIND

COLLECT ALL THE BATTLE BUGS BOOKS!